Alice in Wonderland Coloring Book

LEWIS CARROLL

PICTURES BY
SIR JOHN TENNIEL

[TEXT ABRIDGED]

NEW YORK
DOVER PUBLICATIONS, INC.
LONDON
CONSTABLE & COMPANY LIMITED

Published in Canada by General Publishing Company, Ltd., 30 Lesmill Road, Don Mills, Toronto, Ontario.
Published in the United Kingdom by Constable and Company, Ltd.

Alice in Wonderland Coloring Book is a new work, first published by Dover Publications, Inc., in 1972. The text is abridged from *Alice's Adventures in Wonderland,* originally published by Macmillan and Company in London in 1865, and the illustrations are a selection from Sir John Tenniel's illustrations for that edition. The text was abridged especially for this Dover edition.

DOVER *Pictorial Archive* SERIES

International Standard Book Number: 0-486-22853-3

Manufactured in the United States of America
Dover Publications, Inc.
31 East 2nd Street
Mineola, N.Y. 11501

Alice in Wonderland

ALICE WAS BEGINNING TO GET VERY TIRED of sitting by her sister on the bank and of having nothing to do: once or twice she had peeped into the book her sister was reading, but it had no pictures or conversations in it, "and what is the use of a book," thought Alice, "without pictures or conversations?" Suddenly a White Rabbit with pink eyes ran close by her.

There was nothing so *very* remarkable in that; nor did Alice think it so *very* much out of the way to hear the Rabbit say to itself "Oh dear! Oh dear! I shall be too late!" but when the Rabbit actually *took a watch out of its waistcoat-pocket* and looked at it, and then hurried on, Alice started to her feet, for it flashed across her mind that she had never before seen a rabbit with either a waistcoat-pocket, or a watch to take out of it, and burning with curiosity, she ran across the field after it, and was just in time to see it pop down a large rabbit-hole under the hedge.

In another moment down went Alice after it, never once considering how in the world she was to get out again...

Down, down, down. Would the fall never come to an end? "I wonder how many miles I've fallen by this time?" she said aloud. "I wonder if I shall fall right *through* the earth! How funny it'll seem to come out among the people that walk with their heads downwards! Please, Ma'am, is this New Zealand?" She was trying to curtsey as she spoke — fancy *curtseying* as you're falling through the air! when suddenly, thump! thump! down she came upon a heap of sticks and dry leaves, and the fall was over.

Alice was not a bit hurt. Before her was another long passage, and the White Rabbit was hurrying down it, but when she turned the corner, he was no longer to be seen. She found herself in a long, low hall, lit up by a row of lamps.

There were doors all round the hall, but they were all locked. She wondered how she was ever to get out again.

Suddenly she came upon a little three-legged table, all made of solid glass: there was nothing on it but a tiny golden key, and Alice's first idea was that this might belong to one of the doors of the hall; but alas! either the locks were too large, or the key was too small. However, on the second time round, she came upon a low curtain she had not noticed before, and behind it was a little door about fifteen inches high: she tried the little golden key in the lock, and to her great delight it fitted!

Alice opened the door and found that it led into a small passage, not much larger than a rathole: she knelt down and looked along the passage into the loveliest garden you ever saw. How she longed to get out of that dark hall, and wander about among those beds of bright flowers and those cool fountains, but she could not even get her head through the doorway; "and even if my head would go through," thought poor Alice, "it would be of very little use without my shoulders."

When she went back to the table, she found a little bottle on it ("which certainly was not here before," said Alice), and tied round the neck of the bottle was a paper label, with the words *Drink Me* beautifully printed on it in large letters.

Since the bottle was not marked "poison," Alice ventured to taste it, and, finding it very nice, she very soon finished it off....

"What a curious feeling!" said Alice. "I must be shutting up like a telescope!"

And so it was indeed; she was now only ten inches high, and her face brightened up at the thought that she was now the right size for going through the little door into that lovely garden. But when she got to the door, she found that she had forgotten the little golden key, and when she went back to the table for it, she found she could not possibly reach it. She tried her best to climb up one of the legs of the table, but it was too slippery; and when she had tired herself out with trying, the poor little thing sat down and cried.

"Come, there's no use in crying like that!" said Alice to herself rather sharply. She generally gave herself very good advice and was fond of pretending to be two people. "But it's no use now," thought poor Alice, "to pretend to be two people! Why, there's hardly enough of me left to make *one* respectable person!"

Soon her eye fell on a little glass box that was lying under the table: she opened it, and found in it a very small cake, on which the words *"Eat Me"* were beautifully marked in currants. "Well, I'll eat it," said Alice, "and if it makes me grow larger, I can reach the key; and if it makes me grow smaller I can creep under the door. Which way? Which way?" She set to work, and very soon finished off the cake.

"Curiouser and curiouser!" cried Alice. "Now I'm opening out like the largest telescope that ever was! Good-bye, feet!" (for when she looked down at her feet they seemed to be almost out of sight, they were getting so far off). "Oh, my poor little feet, I wonder who will put on your shoes and stockings for you now, dears?"

Just at this moment her head struck against the roof of the hall: in fact she was now rather more than nine feet high, and she at once took up the little golden key and hurried off to the garden door.

Poor Alice! It was as much as she could do, lying down on one side, to look through into the garden with one eye; but to get through was more hopeless than ever: she sat down and began to cry again.

"You ought to be ashamed of yourself," said Alice, "a great girl like you," (she might well say this), "to go on crying in this way! Stop this moment, I tell you!" But she went on all the same, shedding gallons of tears, until there was a large pool all around her, about four inches deep and reaching half down the hall.

After a time she heard a little pattering of feet in the distance, and hastily dried her eyes. It was the White Rabbit returning, with a pair of white kid-gloves in one hand and a large fan in the other. "Oh! The Duchess! the Duchess! Oh! *Won't* she be savage if I've kept her waiting!"

"If you please, Sir—" said Alice.

The Rabbit started violently, dropped the white kid-gloves and the fan, and scurried away into the darkness as hard as he could go.

Alice took up the fan and gloves, and as the hall was very hot, she began fanning herself. She was surprised to see that she had put on one of the Rabbit's little white kid-gloves. "How can I have done that?" she thought. "I must be getting small again." She got up and went to the table to measure herself by it; she was now about two feet high, and was going on shrinking rapidly. She soon found out that the cause of this was the fan she was holding, and she dropped it hastily, just in time to save herself from shrinking away altogether.

"That was a narrow escape!" said Alice. "And now for the garden!" But alas! the little door was shut again, and the little golden key was lying on the glass table as before, "and things are worse than ever," thought the poor child, "for I never was so small as this before, never!"

As she said these words her foot slipped, and in another moment, splash! she was up to her chin in salt-water. Her first idea was that

she had fallen into the sea; however, she soon made out that she was in the pool of tears she had wept when she was nine feet high.

"I wish I hadn't cried so much!" said Alice, as she swam about, trying to find her way out. "I shall be punished for it now, I suppose, by being drowned in my own tears!"

Just then she heard something splashing about in the pool a little way off, and she soon made out that it was a mouse, that had slipped in like herself.

"Would it be of any use now," thought Alice, "to speak to this mouse?" She began: "O Mouse, do you know the way out of this pool?" (Alice thought this must be the right way of speaking to a mouse: she remembered having seen, in her brother's Latin Grammar, "A Mouse — of a mouse — to a mouse — O mouse!")

"Perhaps it doesn't understand English," thought Alice. "I daresay it's a French mouse, come over with William the Conqueror." So she began again: "Où est ma chatte?" which was the first sentence in her French lesson-book. The Mouse gave a sudden leap out of the water at this mention of cats, and when Alice spoke about dogs, the Mouse began swimming away from her as hard as it could go.

By now the pool was getting quite crowded with the birds and animals that had fallen into it: a Dodo and an Eaglet, and several other curious creatures. Alice led the way, and the whole party swam to the shore.

The first question was how they were all to get dry again: the birds and animals had a consultation about this, and after a few minutes it seemed quite natural to Alice to find herself talking familiarly with them.

At last the Mouse, who seemed to be a person of some authority among them, called out, "Sit down, all of you, and listen to me!

I'll soon make you dry enough!" They all sat down in a large ring, with the Mouse in the middle.

"Are you all ready?" the Mouse said. "This is the driest thing I know. '...William the Conqueror, whose cause was favoured by the pope, was soon submitted to by the English...'"

"That doesn't seem to be drying me," complained Alice.

"The best thing to dry us," the Dodo said, "would be a Caucus-race."

"What *is* a Caucus-race?" asked Alice.

"The best way to explain it is to do it." The Dodo then marked out a race-course, in a sort of circle, and placed everyone along it, here and there. They all began running when they liked, and left off when they liked. At the end of half an hour, when everyone was quite dry, the Dodo called out suddenly, "The race is over!" "But who has won?" everybody said.

"Why," said the Dodo, "everyone has won, and all must have prizes."

"But who is to give the prizes?"

"Why she, of course," the Dodo said, pointing to Alice. Alice put her hand in her pocket and found a box of comfits (luckily the salt-water had not got into it) and handed them round as prizes.

"But she must have a prize herself," said the Mouse.

"Of course," said the Dodo. "What else do you have in your pocket?"

"Only a thimble," said Alice. She handed it to the Dodo, who then handed it back saying "We beg your acceptance of this elegant thimble."

Alice thought the whole thing quite absurd, but they all looked so grave she didn't dare laugh. "I only wish my cat Dinah were here to see it," she said, but at this mention of a cat the birds, making different excuses, scattered as fast as possible in all directions.

The White Rabbit now came tripping slowly back, muttering "The Duchess! The Duchess! Where *can* I have dropped them, I wonder?" Alice guessed that he was looking for the fan and gloves, but they were nowhere to be seen.

"Why, Mary Ann," he said when he saw Alice, "what are you doing out here? Go home this moment, and fetch me a pair of gloves and a fan!" Alice was so frightened that she ran off at once in the direction it pointed to, without trying to explain the mistake that it had made.

"He took me for his housemaid," she said to herself as she ran. "How surprised he'll be when he finds out who I am! But I'd better take him his fan and gloves—that is, if I can find them." As she said this, she came upon a neat little house, on the door of which was a bright brass plate with the name "W. RABBIT" engraved upon it. She went in without knocking, and hurried upstairs, in great fear lest she should meet the real Mary Ann, and be turned out of the house before she had found the fan and gloves.

She was standing in a tidy little room with a table in the window, and on it a fan and two or three pairs of tiny white kid-gloves; she took up the fan and a pair of the gloves, and was just going to leave the room, when her eye fell upon a little bottle that stood near the looking-glass. She uncorked it and put it to her lips. "I know *something* interesting is sure to happen," she said to herself. "I do hope it'll make me grow large again, for really I'm quite tired of being such a tiny little thing!"

It did so indeed, and much sooner than she had expected: before she had drunk half the bottle, she found her head pressing against the ceiling, and had to stoop to save her neck from being broken. "I wish I hadn't drunk quite so much!"

Alas! It was too late to wish that! She went on growing and growing, and very soon had to kneel down on the floor: in another minute there was not even room for this, and she tried the effect of

lying down with one elbow against the door, and the other arm curled round her head. Still she went on growing, and, as a last resource, she put one arm out of the window, and one foot up the chimney, and said to herself "Now I can do no more, whatever happens. What *will* become of me?"

After a few minutes, after she stopped growing, she heard a voice outside. "Mary Ann!" said the voice. "Fetch me my gloves this moment!" Then came a little pattering of feet on the stairs. Alice knew it was the Rabbit coming to look for her, and she trembled till she shook the house, quite forgetting that she was now about a thousand times as large as the Rabbit.

Presently the Rabbit came up to the door, and tried to open it; but, as the door opened inwards, and Alice's elbow was pressed hard against it, that attempt proved a failure. Alice heard it say to itself "Then I'll go round and get in at the window."

"*That* you won't!" thought Alice, and, after waiting till she fancied she heard the Rabbit just under the window, she suddenly spread out her hand, and made a snatch in the air. She heard a little shriek and a fall, and a crash of broken glass.

Next came an angry voice, and someone saying "Now tell me what's that in the window?"

"Sure it's an arm, yer honour."

"An arm, you goose! Who ever saw one that size? Why, it fills the whole window!"

"Well, it's got no business there; go and take it away."

At last Alice spread out her hand again, and made another snatch in the air. This time there were *two* little shrieks, and more sounds of broken glass. "As for pulling me out of the window," Alice thought, "I only wish *they could*! I'm sure I don't want to stay here any longer!"

She waited for some time without hearing anything more; at last came a rumbling of cartwheels, and the sound of many voices: "Here, Bill! The master says you've got to go down the chimney!"

"Oh! So Bill's got to come down the chimney, has he?" said Alice to herself. "I wouldn't be in Bill's place for a good deal: this fire-place is narrow, but I *think* I can kick a little!"

She waited till she heard a little animal scratching and scrambling about in the chimney close above her: then she gave one sharp kick, and waited to see what would happen next.

"Something come at me like a Jack-in-the-Box," someone said, panting, "and up I goes like a sky-rocket!" "That must be Bill," Alice thought.

"We must burn the house down!" said the Rabbit's voice. And Alice called out, as loud as she could, "If you do, I'll set my cat Dinah on you!"

There was a dead silence instantly; then Alice heard the Rabbit say "A barrowful will do, to begin with."

"A barrowful of *what?*" thought Alice. But she had not long to doubt, for the same moment a shower of little pebbles came rattling in at the window, and some of them hit her in the face. She noticed, with some surprise, that the pebbles were all turning into little cakes as they lay on the floor, and a bright idea came into her head. "If I eat one of these cakes," she thought, "it's sure to make *some* change in my size."

So she swallowed one of the cakes, and was delighted to find that she began shrinking directly. As soon as she was small enough to get through the door, she ran out of the house, and found quite a crowd of little animals and birds waiting outside. The poor little Lizard, Bill, was in the middle, being held up by two guinea-pigs, who were giving it something out of a bottle. They all made a rush at Alice the moment she appeared; but she ran off as hard as she could, and soon found herself safe in a thick wood.

"The first thing I've got to do," said Alice to herself, "is to grow to my right size again; and the second thing is to find my way into that lovely garden." A little sharp bark just over her head made her look up in a great hurry.

An enormous puppy was looking down at her with large round eyes, and feebly stretching out one paw, trying to touch her. "Poor little thing!" said Alice, in a coaxing tone, and she tried hard to whistle to it; but she was terribly frightened that it might be hungry, in which case it would be very likely to eat her in spite of all her coaxing.

Hardly knowing what she did, she picked up a little bit of stick, and held it out to the puppy: whereupon the puppy jumped into the air off all its feet at once, with a yelp of delight, and rushed at the stick: then Alice dodged behind a great thistle, to keep herself from being run over. At last it sat down a good way off, panting, with its tongue hanging out of its mouth.

This seemed to Alice a good opportunity for making her escape: so she set off at once and ran until she was quite tired. "And yet what a dear little puppy it was!" said Alice, as she leant against a buttercup to rest herself, and fanned herself with one of its leaves. "I should have liked teaching it some tricks, if I'd only been the right size! Oh dear! I'd nearly forgotten I've got to grow up again. I suppose I ought to eat or drink something: the great question is 'What?'"

There was a large mushroom growing near her, about the same height as herself; and when she had looked under it, and on both sides of it, and behind it, it occurred to her that she might as well see what was on the top of it.

She peeped over the edge of the mushroom, and her eyes immediately met those of a large blue caterpillar, that was sitting on the top, with its arms folded, quietly smoking a long hookah, and taking not the smallest notice of her or of anything else.

The Caterpillar and Alice looked at each other for some time in silence: at last the Caterpillar took the hookah out of his mouth, and addressed her in a languid, sleepy voice.

"Who are *you?*" said the Caterpillar.

This was not an encouraging opening for a conversation. Alice replied, rather shyly, "I—I hardly know, Sir, just at present—at least I know who I *was* when I got up this morning, but I think I must have changed several times since then."

"What do you mean by that?" said the Caterpillar, sternly. "Explain yourself!"

"I can't explain *myself,* I'm afraid, Sir," said Alice, "because I'm not myself, you see."

"I don't see," said the Caterpillar.

"I'm afraid I can't put it more clearly," Alice replied, very politely, "for I can't understand it myself, to begin with; and being so many different sizes in a day is very confusing."

"It isn't," said the Caterpillar.

"Well, perhaps you haven't found it so yet," said Alice; "but when you have to turn into a chrysalis—you will some day, you know—and then after that into a butterfly, I should think you'll feel it a little queer, won't you?"

"Not a bit," said the Caterpillar.

"All I know is, it would feel very queer to *me.*"

"You!" said the Caterpillar contemptuously. "Who are *you?*"

Alice felt a little irritated at the Caterpillar's making such *very* short remarks. She explained that she had been having trouble remembering things. "And I don't keep the same size for ten minutes together."

"Can't remember what things?" said the Caterpillar.

"Things like '*How doth the little busy bee,*'" Alice replied.

"Repeat '*You are old, Father William,*'" said the Caterpillar. Alice folded her hands, and began:—

"You are old, Father William," the young man said
    "And your hair has become very white;
And yet you incessantly stand on your head —
    Do you think, at your age, it is right?"

"In my youth," Father William replied to his son,
    "I feared it might injure the brain;
But, now that I'm perfectly sure I have none,
    Why, I do it again and again."

"You are old," said the youth, "as I mentioned before,
 And have grown most uncommonly fat;
Yet you turned a back-somersault in at the door—
 Pray, what is the reason of that?"

"In my youth," said the sage, as he shook his grey locks,
 "I kept all my limbs very supple
By the use of this ointment—one shilling the box—
 Allow me to sell you a couple?"

"You are old," said the youth, "and your jaws are too weak
    For anything tougher than suet;
Yet you finished the goose, with the bones and the beak —
    Pray, how did you manage to do it?"

"In my youth," said his father, "I took to the law,
    And argued each case with my wife;
And the muscular strength, which it gave to my jaw
    Has lasted the rest of my life."

"You are old," said the youth, "one would hardly suppose
    That your eye was as steady as ever;
Yet you balanced an eel on the end of your nose —
    What made you so awfully clever?"

"I have answered three questions, and that is enough,"
    Said his father. "Don't give yourself airs!
Do you think I can listen all day to such stuff?
    Be off, or I'll kick you down-stairs!"

"What size do you want to be?" the Caterpillar said, when Alice finished.

"Well, I should like to be a *little* larger, Sir, if you wouldn't mind," said Alice: "three inches is such a wretched height to be."

"It is a very good height indeed!" said the Caterpillar angrily, rearing itself upright as it spoke (it was exactly three inches high). "You'll get used to it in time." Then as it crawled away, it remarked, "One side will make you grow taller, the other side will make you grow shorter."

"One side of *what?*" thought Alice to herself.

"Of the mushroom." In another moment the Caterpillar was out of sight.

"Now which is which?" When she nibbled at the right-hand side she got very small; when she nibbled the left her head towered above the trees. She went to work nibbling on the mushroom, and when she saw a little house in an open space, she brought herself down to nine inches high.

She stood looking at the house and wondering what to do next, when suddenly a footman in livery (with a face like a fish) came running out of the wood and rapped loudly at the door with his knuckles. It was opened by another footman in livery, with large eyes like a frog. Alice crept a little way out of the wood to listen.

The Fish-Footman began by producing from under his arm a great letter, nearly as large as himself, and this he handed over to the other, saying, in a solemn tone, "For the Duchess. An invitation from the Queen to play croquet." The Frog-Footman repeated, "From the Queen. An invitation for the Duchess to play croquet." Then they both bowed low, and their curls got entangled.

There was a most extraordinary noise going on inside the house —a constant howling and sneezing, and every now and then a great crash. Neither of the Footmen seemed the least helpful, so Alice timidly opened the door and went in.

The door led right into a large kitchen, which was full of smoke from one end to the other: the Duchess was sitting on a three-legged stool in the middle, nursing a baby: the cook was leaning over the fire, stirring a large cauldron which seemed to be full of soup.

"There's certainly too much pepper in that soup!" Alice said to herself, as well as she could for sneezing.

There was certainly too much of it in the *air*. Even the Duchess sneezed occasionally; and as for the baby, it was sneezing and howling alternately without a moment's pause. The only two creatures in the kitchen that did *not* sneeze were the cook and a large cat which was lying on the hearth and grinning from ear to ear.

"Please would you tell me," said Alice, "why your cat grins like that?"

"It's a Cheshire-Cat," said the Duchess, "and that's why. Pig!"

She said the last word with such sudden violence that Alice quite jumped; but she saw in another moment that it was addressed to the baby, and not to her, so she took courage, and went on again: "I didn't know that cats *could* grin."

"You don't know much," said the Duchess; "and that's a fact."

At this point the cook took the cauldron of soup off the fire, and set to work throwing everything within her reach at the Duchess and the baby—the fire-irons, saucepans, plates, and dishes. The Duchess took no notice of them.

"Oh, *please* mind what you're doing!" cried Alice, jumping up and down in an agony of terror, as an unusually large saucepan flew past the baby's nose, nearly carrying it off.

"Oh, don't bother me!" said the Duchess. And with that she began nursing her child again, singing a sort of lullaby to it as she did so, and giving it a violent shake at the end of every line:—

> *"Speak roughly to your little boy,*
> *And beat him when he sneezes:*
> *He only does it to annoy,*
> *Because he knows it teases."*

"Here! You may nurse it a bit, if you like!" the Duchess said to Alice, flinging the baby at her as she spoke. "I must go and get ready to play croquet with the Queen."

Alice caught the baby with some difficulty, as it was a queer-shaped little creature, and held out its arms and legs in all directions, "just like a star-fish," thought Alice. The poor little thing was snorting like a steam-engine when she caught it, and kept doubling itself up and grunting. "That's not a proper way of expressing yourself," said Alice.

The baby grunted again, and Alice looked very anxiously into its face. There could be no doubt that it had a *very* turn-up nose, much more like a snout than a real nose.

"If you're going to turn into a pig, my dear," said Alice seriously, "I'll have nothing more to do with you." It grunted again, so violently that she looked down into its face in some alarm. This time there could be *no* mistake about it; it was neither more nor less than a pig, and she felt that it would be quite absurd for her to carry it any further.

So she set the little creature down, and felt quite relieved to see it trot away quietly into the wood. "If it had grown up," she said to herself, "it would have made a dreadfully ugly child; but it makes rather a handsome pig, I think." She was startled to see the Cheshire-Cat sitting on a bough of a tree a few yards off.

"Cheshire-Puss," she began, "which way should I go from here?"

"That depends a good deal on where you want to get to."

"I don't much care where —" said Alice.

"Then it doesn't matter which way you go," said the Cat.

"— so long as I get *somewhere*."

"Oh, you're sure to do that," said the Cat, "if you only walk long enough. In *that* direction," the Cat went on, "lives a Hatter: and in *that* direction lives a March Hare. They're both mad."

"But I don't want to go among mad people," Alice remarked.

"Oh, you can't help that. We're all

mad here. By-the-bye, what became of the baby?"

"It turned into a pig," Alice answered very quietly.

"I thought it would," said the Cat, and vanished. A moment later it was back again, sitting on a branch of a tree.

"Did you say 'pig,' or 'fig'?" said the Cat.

"I said 'pig,'" replied Alice; "and I wish you wouldn't keep appearing and vanishing so suddenly: you make one quite giddy!"

"All right!" said the Cat; and this time it vanished quite slowly, beginning with the end of the tail, and ending with the grin, which remained some time after the rest of it had gone.

"Well! I've often seen a cat without a grin," thought Alice; "but a grin without a cat! It's the most curious thing I ever saw!"

She had not gone much farther before she came in sight of the house of the March Hare. She thought it must be the right house, because the chimneys were shaped like ears and the roof was thatched with fur.

There was a table set out under a tree in front of the house, and the March Hare and the Hatter were having tea at it: a Dormouse was sitting between them, fast asleep, and the other two were using it as a cushion, resting their elbows on it, and talking over its head.

"No room! No room!" they cried out when they saw Alice coming. "There's plenty of room!" said Alice indignantly, and she sat down in a large armchair at one end of the table.

"Have some wine," the March Hare said in an encouraging tone.

"I don't see any wine," Alice said.

"There isn't any," said the March Hare.

"Then it wasn't very civil of you to offer it," said Alice angrily.

"It wasn't very civil of you to sit down without being invited," said the March Hare.

"Your hair wants cutting," said the Hatter.

"You should learn not to make personal remarks," Alice said. "It's very rude."

"And you should say what you mean," the March Hare went on.

"I do," Alice hastily replied; "at least—at least I mean what I say—that's the same thing, you know."

"Not the same thing a bit!" said the Hatter. "You might as well say that 'I see what I eat' is the same thing as 'I eat what I see.' What day of the month is it?" he went on, looking at his watch and holding it to his ear.

Alice considered a little. "The fourth."

"Two days wrong!" sighed the Hatter. "I told you butter wouldn't suit the works!" he added, looking angrily at the March Hare.

"It was the *best* butter," the March Hare meekly replied.

"What a funny watch!" Alice remarked. "It tells the day of the month, and doesn't tell what o'clock it is!"

"Why should it?" muttered the Hatter. "Does *your* watch tell you what year it is?"

"Of course not," Alice replied: "but that's because it stays the same year for such a long time together."

"Which is just the same with *mine*," said the Hatter.

"Wake up, Dormouse!" the March Hare shouted, pouring tea on its nose, as the Hatter started to sing:

> *"Twinkle, twinkle, little bat!*
> *How I wonder what you're at!*
> *Up above the world you fly,*
> *Like a tea tray in the sky.*
> *Twinkle, twinkle—"*

("Twinkle, twinkle, twinkle, twinkle—" sang the Dormouse sleepily.)

"I should think," Alice said, "you could find something better to do with your time—"

"Time?" the Hatter said. "We've nothing to do with Time. It's always six o'clock here."

"Is that the reason so many tea things are put out?" Alice asked.

"Yes, it's always tea-time, and we've no time to wash the things between whiles."

"Then you keep moving round, I suppose?"

"Exactly so," said the Hatter: "as the things get used up."

"Take some more tea," the March Hare said to Alice.

"I've had nothing yet," Alice replied in an offended tone: "so I can't take more."

"You mean you can't take less," said the Hatter: "it's very easy to take *more* than nothing. I want a clean cup," he went on: "let's all move one place on."

He moved on as he spoke, and the Dormouse followed him: the March Hare moved into the Dormouse's place, and Alice rather

unwillingly took the place of the March Hare, who had just upset the milk-jug.

"I don't think—" Alice began.

"Then you shouldn't talk," said the Hatter.

This piece of rudeness was more than Alice could bear: she got up in great disgust, and walked off: the Dormouse fell asleep instantly, and the last time she saw the other two, they were trying to put the Dormouse into the teapot.

"At any rate I'll never go *there* again!" said Alice. "It's the stupidest tea-party I ever was at in all my life!"

Just as she said this, she noticed that one of the trees had a door leading right into it. In she went, and once more found herself in the long hall, and close to the little glass table. She began by taking the little golden key, and unlocking the door that led into the garden. Then she went to work nibbling at the mushroom (she had kept a piece of it in her pocket) till she was about a foot high. Then she walked down the little passage: and *then*—she found herself at last in the beautiful garden, among the bright flower-beds and the cool fountains.

A large rose-tree stood near the entrance of the garden: the roses growing on it were white, but there were three gardeners at it, busily painting them red. "Would you mind telling me, please," said Alice, "why you are painting these roses?"

Gardeners *Five* and *Seven* said nothing, but looked at *Two. Two* began in a low voice, "Why, the fact is, you see, Miss, this here ought to have been a *red* rose-tree, and we put a white one in by mistake; and, if the Queen was to find it out, we should all have our heads cut off, you know." At this moment, *Five*, who had been anxiously looking across the garden, called out "The Queen! The Queen!" and the three gardeners instantly threw themselves flat upon their faces.

First came ten soldiers carrying clubs: these were all shaped like the three gardeners, oblong and flat, with their hands and feet at the corners: next the ten courtiers: these were ornamented all over with diamonds. After these came the royal children, ornamented with hearts. Next came the guests, mostly Kings and Queens, and among them Alice recognized the White Rabbit. Then followed the Knave of Hearts, carrying the King's crown on a cushion, and last of all THE KING AND THE QUEEN OF HEARTS.

When the procession came opposite Alice, they all stopped and the Queen said: "Who is this? What's your name, child?"

"My name is Alice, so please your Majesty," said Alice; she added to herself, "Why, they're only a pack of cards, after all. I needn't be afraid of them."

The Queen pointed to the rose trees. "What's going on here?"

"How should I know?" said Alice. "It's no business of *mine*."

The Queen turned crimson with fury, and, after glaring at her for a moment like a wild beast, began screaming "Off with her head! Off with—"

"Nonsense!" said Alice, very loudly and decidedly.

"Can you play croquet?" the Queen asked after a long silence.

"Yes!" shouted Alice.

"Come on, then!" roared the Queen, and Alice joined the procession.

"It's—it's a very fine day!" said a timid voice at her side. She was walking by the White Rabbit, who was peeping anxiously into her face.

"Very," said Alice. "Where's the Duchess?"

"Hush! Hush!" said the Rabbit in a low hurried tone. He looked anxiously over his shoulder and whispered "She's under sentence of execution."

"What for?" said Alice.

"She boxed the Queen's ears—" the Rabbit began. Alice gave a little scream of laughter. "Oh, hush, the Queen will hear you!"

"Get to your places," shouted the Queen in a voice of thunder, and people began running about in all directions: however, they got settled down in a minute or two and the game began.

Alice thought she had never seen such a curious croquet-ground in her life: it was all ridges and furrows: the croquet balls were live hedgehogs, and the mallets live flamingoes, and the soldiers had to double themselves up and stand on their hands and feet to make the arches.

The chief difficulty Alice found at first was in managing her flamingo: she succeeded in getting its body tucked away, comfortably enough under her arm, with its legs hanging down, but generally, just as she had got its neck nicely straightened out, and was going to give the hedgehog a blow with its head, it *would* twist itself round and look up in her face. When she had got its head down, and was going to begin again, it was very provoking to find that the hedgehog had unrolled itself, and was in the act of crawling away.

The players all played at once, without waiting for turns, quarreling all the while, and fighting for the hedgehogs; and in a very short time the Queen was in a furious passion, and went stamping about, and shouting "Off with his head!" about once in a minute.

Alice was looking about for some way of escape, when she was surprised to see the Duchess coming.

"You can't think how glad I am to see you again, you dear old thing!" said the Duchess, as she tucked her arm affectionately into Alice's, and they walked off together.

Alice was very glad to find her in such a pleasant temper, and thought to herself that perhaps it was only the pepper that made her so savage when they met in the kitchen. "Maybe it's always

pepper that makes people hot-tempered," she thought, "and vinegar that makes them sour—and barley-sugar and such things that make children sweet-tempered."

"You're thinking about something, my dear," the Duchess was saying, "and that makes you forget to talk. I'll remember the moral of that in a bit."

"Perhaps it hasn't one," Alice ventured to remark.

"Tut, tut, child!" said the Duchess. "Everything's got a moral, if only you can find it."

Alice did not much like her keeping so close to her, first because the Duchess was *very* ugly; and secondly, because she was exactly the right height to rest her chin on Alice's shoulder, and it was an uncomfortably sharp chin.

"The game's going on rather better now," said Alice, as she put down her flamingo.

"'Tis so," said the Duchess: "and the moral of that is—'Take care of the sense, and the sounds will take care of themselves.'"

"How fond she is of finding morals in things!" Alice thought to herself.

"I make you a present," the Duchess said, "of everything I've said as yet."

"A cheap sort of present!" thought Alice.

To Alice's great surprise, the Duchess's voice died away, and there stood the Queen in front of them, with her arms folded, frowning like a thunder-storm.

"A fine day, your Majesty!" the Duchess began in a low, weak voice.

"Now, I give you fair warning," shouted the Queen; "either you or your head must be off! Take your choice!"

The Duchess took her choice, and was gone in a moment.

"Let's go on with the game," the Queen said to Alice; and Alice was too frightened to say a word. By the end of half an hour, all the players except the King, the Queen, and Alice were under sentence of execution.

Then the Queen left off, and said to Alice, "Have you seen the Mock Turtle yet?"

"No," said Alice. "I don't even know what a Mock Turtle is."

"It's the thing Mock Turtle Soup is made from," said the Queen. "Come on and he shall tell you his history."

As they walked off together, Alice heard the King say in a low voice to the company generally "You are all pardoned." "Come, *that's* a good thing!" she said to herself, for she had felt quite unhappy at the number of executions the Queen had ordered.

They soon came upon a Gryphon, lying fast asleep in the sun. "Up, lazy thing!" said the Queen, "and take this young lady to see the Mock Turtle," and she walked off, leaving Alice alone with the Gryphon.

The Gryphon sat up and rubbed its eyes. "What fun!" it said.

"What *is* the fun?" said Alice.

"Why, *she*," said the Gryphon. "It's all her fancy: they never executes nobody, you know. Come on!"

They had not gone far before they saw the Mock Turtle in the distance, sitting sad and lonely on a little ledge of rock, and, as they came nearer, Alice could hear him sighing as if his heart would break. "What is his sorrow?" she asked the Gryphon. And the Gryphon answered, "It's all his fancy, too: he hasn't got no sorrow, you know."

So they went up to the Mock Turtle, who looked at them with large eyes full of tears, but said nothing.

"This here young lady," said the Gryphon, "she wants to know your history, she do."

"I'll tell it her," said the Mock Turtle in a deep, hollow tone. "Sit down, both of you, and don't speak a word till I've finished."

"Once," the Turtle said, with a deep sigh, "I was a real Turtle." These words were followed by a very long silence, broken only by an occasional "Hjckrrh!" from the Gryphon, and the constant heavy sobbing of the Mock Turtle. "When we were little," he went on, "we went to school in the sea. The master was an old Turtle—we used to call him Tortoise—"

"Why did you call him Tortoise, if he wasn't one?" Alice asked.

"We called him Tortoise because he taught us," said the Mock Turtle angrily. "Really you are very dull." They both looked at poor Alice, who felt ready to sink into the earth.

"We went to school in the sea, though you mayn't believe it—"

"I never said I didn't!" interrupted Alice.

"You did," said the Mock Turtle.

"I've been to a day-school, too," said Alice. "We learned French and music."

"And washing?" said the Mock Turtle.

"Certainly not!" said Alice indignantly.

"Now at *ours*," the Mock Turtle said, "they had 'French, music, *and washing.*'"

"You couldn't have wanted it much," said Alice, "living at the bottom of the sea."

"I couldn't afford to learn it," said the Mock Turtle with a sigh. "I only took the regular course."

"What was that?" inquired Alice.

"Reeling and Writhing, to begin with—and then the different branches of Arithmetic—Ambition, Distraction, Uglification, and Derision."

"What else had you to learn?" said Alice.

"Well, there was Mystery," the Mock Turtle replied. "Mystery, ancient and modern, with Seaography: then Drawling—"

"I went to the Classical master," said the Gryphon. "He was an old crab, *he* was. He taught Laughing and Grief, they used to say."

"And how many hours a day did you do lessons?" said Alice.

"Ten hours the first day; nine the next; and so on."

"What a curious plan!" exclaimed Alice.

"That's the reason they're called lessons," the Gryphon remarked: "because they lessen from day to day."

"That's enough about lessons," he went on. "Tell her about the games now."

Sobs choked the Mock Turtle's voice. "You may not have lived much under the sea, or been introduced to a lobster, or known what a delightful thing a Lobster-Quadrille is!"

"What sort of dance is that?" said Alice.

"Why, you first form into a line along the sea-shore —" Without more ado, the Mock Turtle and the Gryphon began solemnly dancing round Alice (every now and then treading on her toes) as the Mock Turtle sang, very slowly and sadly —

"Will you walk a little faster?" said a whiting to a snail,
"There's a porpoise close behind us, and he's treading on my tail.
See how eagerly the lobsters and the turtles all advance.
They are waiting on the shingle — will you come and join the dance?
  Will you, won't you, will you, won't you, will you join the dance?
  Will you, won't you, will you, won't you, won't you join the dance?"

Alice was glad when the dance was over.

"Do you know why the whiting is called a whiting?" the Gryphon said. "Because it does the boots and shoes."

"Mine are done with blacking —"

"Well, under the sea the boots and shoes are done with whiting."

"And what are they made of?" Alice asked.

"Soles and eels, of course. Any shrimp could have told you that."

At this point the Mock Turtle, once more choked with sobs, began singing again:

> *"Beautiful Soup, so rich and green,*
> *Waiting in a hot tureen!*
> *Who for such dainties would not stoop?*
> *Soup of the evening, beautiful Soup!*
> *Soup of the evening, beautiful Soup!*
>
> *"Beau—ootiful Soo—oop!*
> *Beau—ootiful Soo—oop!*
> *Soo—oop of the e—e—evening,*
> *Beautiful, beautiful Soup!"*

He had just begun to repeat it when a cry "The trial's beginning," was heard in the distance.

"Come on!" cried the Gryphon, taking Alice by the hand before she could ask whose trial it was.

The King and Queen of Hearts were seated on their throne when they arrived, with a great crowd assembled about them—all sorts of little birds and beasts as well as the whole pack of cards: the Knave was standing before them, in front of a table filled with tarts, and near the King was the White Rabbit, holding a trumpet.

Alice had never been in a court of justice before, but she had read about them in books, and she knew nearly everyone there. "That's the Judge," she said to herself, "because of his great wig." The Judge was the King; and as he wore his crown over the wig, he did not look at all comfortable.

"And that's the jury-box," thought Alice; "and those twelve creatures" (some were animals and some were birds) "are the jurors." She said this word two or three times, being rather proud of it.

The twelve jurors (one of whom proved to be Bill the Lizard) were busily writing on slates. "What are they doing?" Alice whispered to the Gryphon.

"They're putting down their names, for fear they should forget them before the end of the trial."

"Herald, read the accusation!" said the King. The White Rabbit blew three blasts on the trumpet, unrolled a scroll, and read:

> *"The Queen of Hearts, she made some tarts,*
> *All on a summer day:*
> *The Knave of Hearts, he stole those tarts*
> *And took them quite away."*

The first witness was the Hatter. He came in with a teacup in one hand and a piece of bread-and-butter in the other. "I beg pardon, your Majesty," he began, "but I hadn't quite finished my tea."

"You ought to have finished. When did you begin?"

The Hatter looked at the March Hare and the Dormouse. "Fourteenth of March, I think it was."

"Fifteenth," said the March Hare.

"Sixteenth," said the Dormouse.

"Write that down," the King said to the jury; and the jury wrote down all three dates on their slates, and then added them up, and reduced the answer to shillings and pence.

"Take off your hat," the King said to the Hatter.

"It isn't mine," said the Hatter.

"*Stolen!*" the King exclaimed.

"I keep them to sell," the Hatter added. "I've none of my own. I'm a hatter." He was trembling so he shook off both his shoes.

Just at this moment Alice felt a curious sensation: she was beginning to grow larger again, but she decided to remain where she was as long as there was room for her.

"I wish you wouldn't squeeze so," said the Dormouse, who was sitting next to her.

"I can't help it," Alice said very meekly. "I'm growing."

"You've got no right to grow *here*."

"Don't talk nonsense," said Alice more boldly: "you know you're growing too."

"Yes, but *I* grow at a reasonable pace," said the Dormouse.

"Give your evidence," the King ordered the Hatter, "or I'll have you executed."

The miserable Hatter dropped his teacup and bread-and-butter and went down on one knee. "I'm a poor man, your Majesty."

"You're a *very* poor *speaker*," said the King. "If that's all you know about it, you may stand down."

"I can't go no lower," said the Hatter: "I'm on the floor, as it is."

"Then you may *sit* down," the King replied.

The Hatter hurriedly left the court, without even waiting to put his shoes on.

"Call the *next* witness," the King said, when the court was cleared again. And he added, in an undertone to the Queen, "Really, my dear, *you* must cross-examine the next witness. It quite makes my forehead ache!"

Imagine Alice's surprise when the White Rabbit read out, at the top of his shrill little voice, "Alice!"

"Here!" cried Alice, quite forgetting in the flurry of the moment how large she had grown, and she jumped up in such a hurry that she tipped over the jury-box with the edge of her skirt, upsetting all the jurymen on the heads of the crowd below.

"Oh, I beg your pardon!" she exclaimed in a tone of great dismay, and began picking them up again as quickly as she could.

As soon as the jury had recovered from the shock, and their slates

and pencils had been handed back to them, the King turned to Alice. "What do you know about this business?"

"Nothing," said Alice.

"Nothing *whatever?*" persisted the King.

"Nothing whatever," said Alice.

"That's very important," the King said, turning to the jury. They were just beginning to write this down when the White Rabbit interrupted: "*Un*important, your Majesty means, of course."

"*Un*important, of course, I meant," the King said. Some of the jury wrote down "important" and some "unimportant."

"Silence!" the King called out, and read from his book: "Rule Forty-two. *All persons more than a mile high to leave the court.*"

Everybody looked at Alice.

"I'm not a mile high," said Alice.

"You are," said the King.

"Nearly two miles high," added the Queen.

"Well, I shan't go, at any rate; besides, that's not a regular rule: you invented it just now."

"It's the oldest rule in the book," said the King.

"Then it ought to be Number One," said Alice.

The King turned pale, and shut his note-book hastily. "Consider your verdict," he said to the jury, in a low trembling voice.

"There's more evidence to come yet, please your Majesty," said the White Rabbit. "This paper has just been picked up." There was dead silence in the court, whilst the White Rabbit read: —

> *"They told me you had been to her,*
> *And mentioned me to him:*
> *She gave me a good character,*
> *But said I could not swim.*

My notion was that you had been
(Before she had this fit)
An obstacle that came between
Him, and ourselves, and it..."

"That's the most important evidence yet," said the King.

"If anyone can explain it," said Alice (she had grown so large in the last few minutes that she wasn't a bit afraid of interrupting him). "*I* don't believe there's an atom of meaning in it."

"If there's no meaning," said the King, "that saves a world of trouble." He spread out the verses on his knee. "And yet—" he hesitated—"'*said I could not swim*—' you can't swim, can you?" he added, turning to the Knave.

The Knave shook his head sadly. "Do I look like it?" he said. (Which he certainly did *not*, being made entirely of cardboard.)

"Then again," said the King—"'*before she had this fit*'—you never had *fits*, my dear, I think?" he said of the Queen.

"Never!" said the Queen, furiously.

"Then the words don't *fit* you," said the King, smiling. "Let the jury consider their verdict."

"No, no!" said the Queen. "Sentence first—verdict afterwards."

"Stuff and nonsense!" said Alice loudly. "The idea of having the sentence first!"

"Hold your tongue!" said the Queen, turning purple.

"I won't!" said Alice.

"Off with her head!" the Queen shouted. Nobody moved.

"Who cares for *you*?" said Alice (she had grown to her full size by this time). "You're nothing but a pack of cards!"

At this the whole pack rose up into the air, and came flying down upon her; she gave a little scream, half of fright and half of anger, and tried to beat them off, and found herself lying on the bank, with her head on the lap of her sister.

"Oh, I've had such a curious dream!" said Alice. And she told her sister all these strange Adventures of hers. And when she had finished, her sister kissed her, and said "It was a curious dream, dear, certainly; but now run in to your tea: it's getting late." And Alice got up and ran off, thinking while she ran, what a wonderful dream it had been, one she would remember years from now as a dream of Wonderland of long ago.